MAR 0 9 2018

A THIRST FOR HOME

A Story of Water across the World

Christine Ieronimo

ILLUSTRATIONS BY
Eric Velasquez

BLOOMSBURY
NEW YORK LONDON OXFORD NEW DELHI SYDNEY

First published in the United States of America in May 2014
by Walker Books for Young Readers, an imprint of Bloomsbury Publishing, Inc.
www.bloomsbury.com

Bloomsbury is a registered trademark of Bloomsbury Publishing Plc

For information about permission to reproduce selections from this book, write to
Permissions, Bloomsbury Children's Books, 1385 Broadway, New York, New York 10018
Bloomsbury books may be purchased for business or promotional use. For information on bulk purchases please contact
Macmillan Corporate and Premium Sales Department at specialmarkets@macmillan.com

Library of Congress Cataloging-in-Publication Data
Ieronimo, Christine.
A thirst for home : a story of water across the world / by Christine Ieronimo ; illustrated by Eric Velasquez.
pages   cm
Summary: Alemitu lives with her mother in a poor village in Ethiopia, where she must walk miles for water and hunger
roars in her belly. Even though life is difficult, she dreams of someday knowing more about the world. When her mother
has no choice but to leave her at an orphanage to give her a chance at a better life, an American family adopts Alemitu.
Includes bibliographical references.
ISBN 978-0-8027-2307-9 (hardcover) • ISBN 978-0-8027-2308-6 (reinforced)
[1. Water supply—Fiction. 2. Ethiopia—Fiction. 3. Intercountry adoption—Fiction. 4. Adoption—Fiction.] I. Title.
PZ7.I23Th 2014   [E]—dc23   2013039001

Art created with mixed media and oil on watercolor paper
Typeset in Brioso Pro
Book design by Nicole Gastonguay
Printed in China by C&C Offset Printing Co., Ltd., Shenzhen, Guangdong
3 5 7 9 10 8 6 4 2 (hardcover)
1 3 5 7 9 10 8 6 4 2 (reinforced)

All papers used by Bloomsbury Publishing, Inc., are natural, recyclable products
made from wood grown in well-managed forests. The manufacturing processes
conform to the environmental regulations of the country of origin.

For Aunt Maria —C. I.

For Jordan and Liz —E. V.

When I was **Alemitu** (ah-le-*mee*-too), my name
meant *world*. I lived with my *emaye*, or mama, in a small
village in Ethiopia. The sun was always smiling down on
me and whispered my name with its hot, sticky breath.

Emaye and I often went to the watering hole. We walked all morning with the blazing orange sun on our backs. Emaye told me a story while we walked. "Our watering hole gives us something precious," she said, "even more precious than gold. We could live a lifetime without gold but not a day without a drink of water. All over the world, the clouds make the rain and the rain brings us our water. This connects us to everyone and everywhere. Water is life."

Finally, we arrived at the watering
hole and Emaye filled her jug.
When I looked down into the
water, I saw myself in the stillness.
I tried to see the bottom, but it was
dark and deep. *How deep?* I wondered.
What mysteries are hidden beneath? As
I leaned down to take a drink, the water
rippled and winked at me. I imagined a
secret passage that connected to a place I had
never been. Maybe someday I would find out
what was on the other side.

We walked home barefoot through the brown patches of grass and dry, cracked earth. My feet are scarred from walking many miles. They are rough but strong. They have carried me far with bundles of wood strapped to my back, even as the fierce lion roared in my belly.

That night I lay next to Emaye on our mat of woven leaves. It felt soft under my tired limbs. Our food had run out, and in the darkness the lion roared his loudest. I tried to ignore it, snuggling close to Emaye's warmth, and I finally fell asleep.

One day Emaye took me to a place where she said the lion in my belly would never roar again. "Soon you will find out what is on the other side, but I cannot go with you," she said. Emaye cried, and her tears were like raindrops so precious that I tried to collect them with the scarf she gave me. But there were too many, and together we cried a shower of tears.

Before she left, Emaye kissed me and told me that she loved me forever. *"Ehwatdeshahlehu, se't lidj."* (I love you, daughter.)

In this new place I waited every day for Emaye to return. I held the scarf full of her precious raindrops, wondering how I could find the secrets of the watering hole here. I didn't know that this was just the beginning of my journey.

A lady the color of the moon came to visit me one day many weeks later. The nannies told me she was my new emaye. She sat with me at lunch and helped me eat my steaming orange stew. Together we found the best part, the hard-boiled egg. It was the grand prize.

She spoke with words I did not understand, but she stayed and held me on her lap until I fell asleep. I felt safe again.

Now I am Eva. My name means *life*.

I have traveled far to a new home. I have a sister, two
brothers, a dad, and a mom who is never far. Here the
wind whispers my name with its crisp, cool sigh.

Each morning when I get up, I take a drink of water
that is always cold and clean. I drink every last drop. I
think of Emaye and wish I could show her.

Here, I never have to walk very far,
but my feet carry me to new places.
My bundle of wood has been replaced
with a backpack filled with books and
other treasures.

Today I am going on a picnic with my family. I have on my new shoes, which I am glad for, but sometimes when I look down, I miss my feet. They are hidden inside and want to come out. I want to show them to the world. I am proud of my feet, which have carried me far. I take off my shoes and run through the grass.

The soft green tickles my toes and my heels. The sun follows me with every step. Since I have come here the lion roaring in my belly isn't fierce anymore. He isn't even roaring. I eat my whole sandwich, even the crust, because I am afraid one day he will come back.

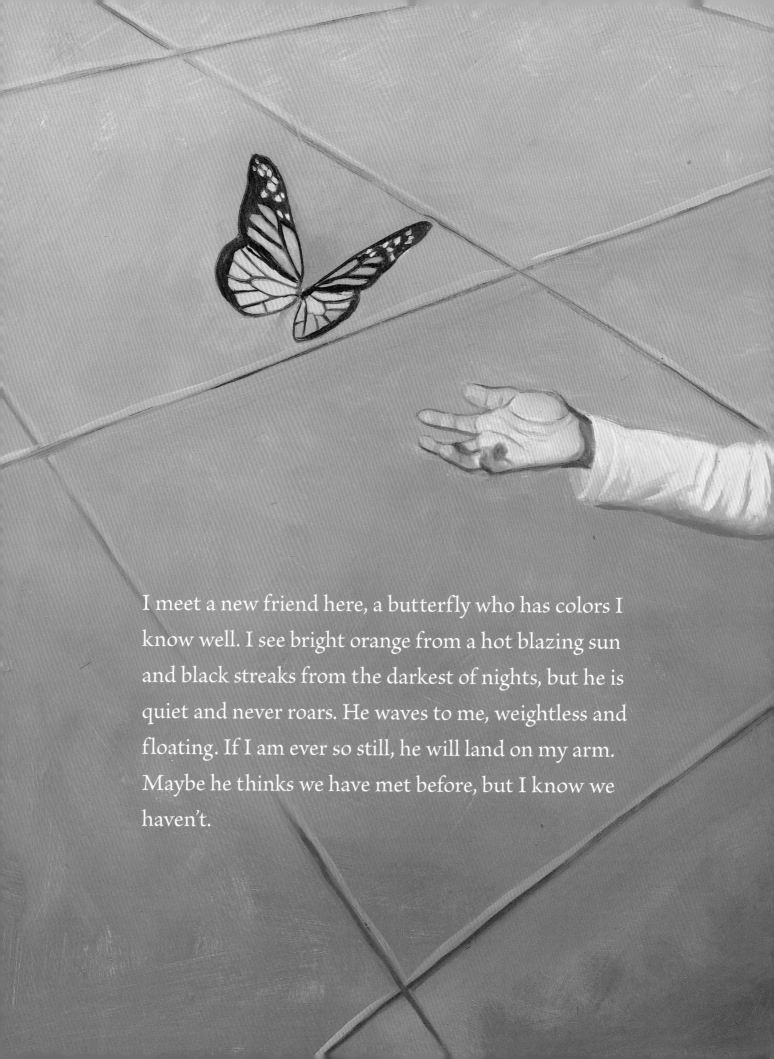

I meet a new friend here, a butterfly who has colors I know well. I see bright orange from a hot blazing sun and black streaks from the darkest of nights, but he is quiet and never roars. He waves to me, weightless and floating. If I am ever so still, he will land on my arm. Maybe he thinks we have met before, but I know we haven't.

That night, I hear the raindrops banging on the roof. I remember what Emaye said, that the water connects us all. I toss and turn and finally crawl into bed between Mom and Dad. I feel safe, like the smallest twig in my bundle of wood.

In the morning, the rain has stopped.
Outside is the biggest, most beautiful
puddle shimmering in the sun. When I
look down, I am amazed at what I see.
It invites me to take a drink, so I cup my
hands, bend down close.

It is at that moment that I realize
where I am—on the other side of our watering
hole. I see Emaye smiling. The water has connected
my two worlds, and I know who I am.

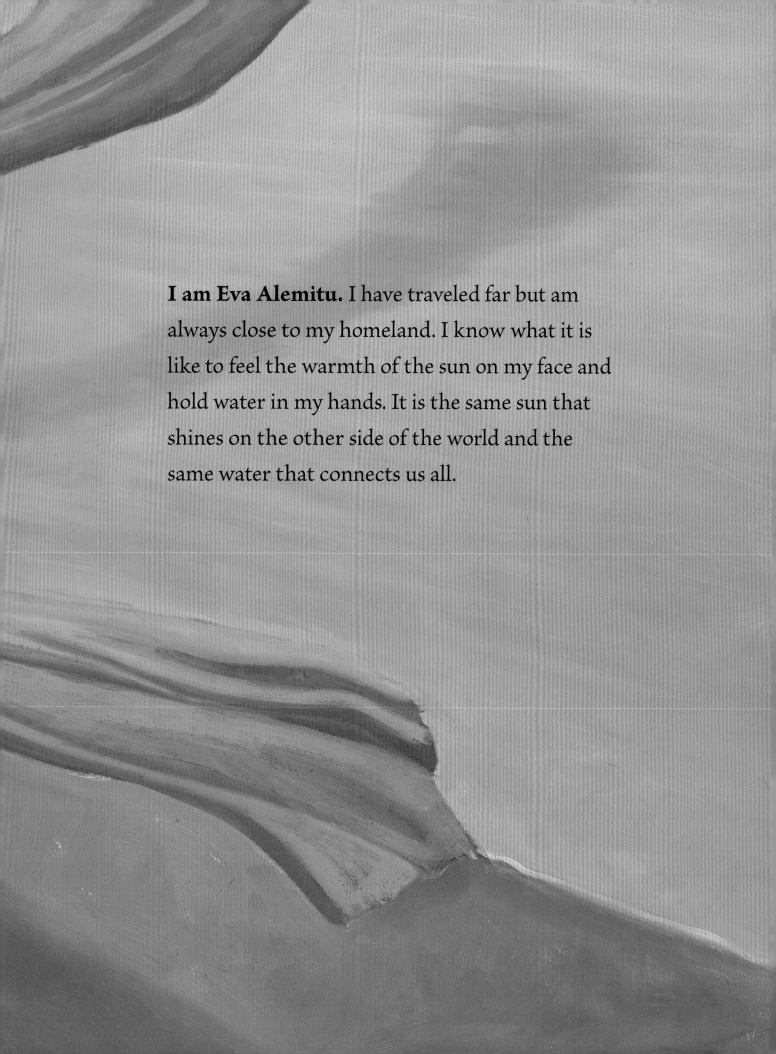

I am Eva Alemitu. I have traveled far but am always close to my homeland. I know what it is like to feel the warmth of the sun on my face and hold water in my hands. It is the same sun that shines on the other side of the world and the same water that connects us all.